Playoffs

Playoffs

Stefan Kowalski

Strategic Book Publishing and Rights Co.

Strategic Book Publishing & Rights Co., LLC
USA | Singapore
www.sbpra.net

For information about special discounts for bulk purchases, please contact Strategic Book Publishing and Rights Co. Special Sales, at bookorder@sbpra.net.

ISBN: 978-1-951530-99-0

Dedication

To my daughters who were the inspiration for this book

CHAPTER 1

The minute the school day ended, Peyton grabbed her backpack and sprinted home. Peyton Alyssa Washburn, who was fast to begin with, ran faster that day than any other day in the past. At four feet four inches tall and only fifty-two pounds, Peyton was relatively short and thin for a fourth grader, but she was very fast. She ran the four blocks in five minutes.

"Dad, you'll never guess what happened today!" Peyton said, gasping for air as she sprinted into the house. Peyton's father, who had arrived home only a few minutes earlier, had just finished changing out of his work clothes and emerged from the bedroom.

"What happened, sweetie?"

"Coach Anderson wants me to try out for the team this year."

Coach Anderson was the middle school girls' basketball coach and a former college All-American at Syracuse University. During her time playing in college, she was a fierce competitor who made up for her lack of size with speed and aggressiveness. This was her first year at the middle school, and she had a reputation for being a no-nonsense kind of coach.

"What do you mean she asked you to tryout for the middle school team? I didn't think fourth graders were allowed to tryout for the middle school sports teams." Dad continued staring at his daughter with a look of puzzlement.

"I didn't think they could either, but coach came to school today and talked to me during recess. She said that she has seen me play and thinks that I have a chance to make the team. Tryouts are in two weeks," Peyton said with a smile that was as bright as the sun.

"Peyton, slow down and take a breath. Before any decision is made, let's sit down tonight after dinner and talk with Mom about this. There is a lot to think about before it's a done deal."

Even before he got the words out of his mouth, Peyton's father knew that his daughter would be trying out for the middle school girls' basketball team. His daughter loved basketball and had become a very good player at a young age, primarily because of his influence on her. When he found out that his wife was pregnant and they were having a daughter, he immediately began decorating her nursery with stuffed basketballs, college and professional team mascots and logos, and even a framed New York Liberty WNBA basketball jersey. He hoped that if his daughter woke up every morning and saw the jersey on the wall it would entice her into playing the sport someday.

He got his wish. Peyton had been playing basketball ever since she could walk. He continued to develop her interest in the sport by bringing her to local college men's and women's basketball games and sitting courtside so she could experience the game up close. Early on, he also coached her on how to play and think on the court. All of this influence had greatly affected his daughter. She had become a well-known, young basketball star at an early age in the community.

Peyton had been playing in leagues and tournaments ever since she was six years old. She had numerous MVP trophies and Most Outstanding Player awards littered around her bedroom. She loved the game and always wanted to compete against girls or boys who were older than she was, because she loved the competition. She inherited this competitiveness from her father. Peyton's father had himself been an outstanding basketball player when he was younger. He earned a basketball scholarship at a division two school and was the starting point guard for three seasons until a knee injury ended his competitive playing days.

The fact that Coach Anderson wanted her to tryout against middle school girls, Peyton's father knew that there was no doubt that Peyton was going to insist that she tryout, but the rules in the house were that any major decision be made as a family. So, that night after dinner, Peyton, Dad, and Mom discussed the idea.

"Your father told me what Coach Anderson said to you today, and he and I have talked about it," Mom said. "Before you make any final decision, you need to think about all the factors that are involved. First, you're going to be two or three years younger, and a few inches shorter, than the other girls on the team. Also, none of those girls are your friends, and it's not going to be the same as it has been in the past when you've always been with girls you know."

"Another thing you're going to have to think about is that the girls are probably not going to like you," Dad chimed in.

"What do you mean they're not going to like me?" Peyton questioned.

"Well, think about it. You are a younger player who is competing against them for a spot on the team and playing time. They don't know you, and they will probably see you as a threat," Dad continued. "You also need to understand that there is no guarantee you'll make the team. Remember, it's called a tryout for a reason."

Peyton dropped her head and nodded, acknowledging that she understood what her parents were telling her.

"Now listen very carefully," her father continued. "You know that Mom and I will support any decision you ultimately make. We just want to make sure you fully understand that if you do decide to try out, these are some of the factors you will have to consider. I'll call Coach Anderson and get the details about when tryouts start and where they're going to be located. You take a day or two to think about what Mom and I explained, and let us know what you want to do."

Before her dad had even finished his sentence, Peyton knew what she was going to do. She had always looked forward to competition, and this was no different. In fact, this was the ultimate challenge. She was going to try out, and she was going to make the girls' middle school basketball team.

CHAPTER 2

Beginning the next day, Peyton practiced harder than she had ever practiced before. The weather outside was beautiful, so she was able to spend most of her time at the local park, which was only two blocks away. Peyton loved spending time at the park. It was often deserted, and Peyton knew that she could practice without interruption. It was quiet, and there weren't the distractions of her friends in the neighborhood riding bicycles, rollerblading, and stopping by unannounced to hang out. Besides, the park was her haven. It was where her dad brought her to practice on a regulation court because their driveway was too small for an acceptable practice facility.

While at the park, Peyton worked on her ball-handling skills by setting up orange cones the length of the court and weaving in and out of them while dribbling the basketball with her right and left hands. After the ball handling, Peyton worked on her jump shots. She first practiced shooting from distances of five feet from the basket, then moving ten feet away, and finally moving out to the three-point line, which is eighteen feet, nine inches from the basket.

After Peyton felt she had worked enough on jump shooting, she moved on to endurance. She practiced running the length of the court, touching the end line, and then running to the opposite end of the court and touching the end line. She repeated the process over and over until she collapsed from exhaustion. While she lay in the middle of the basketball court gasping for air, she thought, *I know this will get me ready.*

Over the course of the next couple of weeks, Peyton could be found at the park every day after school, practicing and preparing for tryouts.

CHAPTER 3

With the tryouts only a few days away, nervous anticipation began setting in.

"I haven't been feeling very well the last few days," Peyton announced at dinner one evening.

"What's wrong?" Mom replied.

"My stomach just feels off. I'm not really hungry, and I have a constant upset stomach feeling," Peyton responded.

"You're just a little nervous, dear," Dad piped in. "You know that tryouts are in a few days, and you're getting a little anxious. It's a very normal feeling, and it's nothing to worry about. Once you step on the basketball court, you'll forget all about being nervous and you'll be fine. Remember last summer before the league championship game when you had the same feelings? You went out and had the game of your life!"

"Oh yeah. I guess it is the same kind of feeling," Peyton replied.

"Just make sure you eat," said Mom. "You need your energy."

Although the nervous stomach continued to bother Peyton, she ate like her mom asked. She knew she needed energy if she was to be at the top of her game come tryouts.

The night before the tryout, Peyton couldn't sleep. She kept thinking about making the team and how amazing it would be to play against all those older girls. Finally, after hours of thinking and wondering about the tryouts, Peyton fell asleep.

The alarm startled her out of bed, and although she had only slept for a few hours, she was wide awake and eager to get the day going. After taking a shower, she made her way downstairs, where Mom and Dad were already at the kitchen table. Mom was grading papers for her fourth-grade students, and Dad was reading the paper.

"Hey, champ. Excited about practice today?" Dad asked.

"Yup," Peyton quickly answered, "I couldn't sleep last night because I am so ready to just get out there and play."

"Well, why don't you sit down and have some breakfast. I'll make you some eggs and toast," Mom said. "And another thing, I better not get a call from Mrs. Shankos telling me that you weren't paying attention during class because you're daydreaming about practice or something. You know the rules: academics before athletics."

After breakfast, Peyton grabbed her gym bag, which was loaded with her basketball sneakers and her favorite leather basketball, kissed her mom and dad, and left the house to begin walking to school. *How do Mom and Dad expect me to concentrate in school today when I have such an important practice later?* Peyton thought to herself. *I just have to get through these next six hours, and then I get to play.*

That school day was the longest Peyton ever remembered. Even recess seemed to go by slowly. Finally, the end of the day came, and Peyton packed up her backpack and headed next door to the middle school. All of the neighborhood schools were located adjacent to one another on the same campus. Holland Elementary School had grades kindergarten through sixth, Holland Middle School was grades seven through eight, and Holland High School was for grades nine through twelve.

Walking through the gymnasium door, Peyton could feel her heart racing. Looking around, she saw Coach Anderson and another adult standing underneath one of the baskets talking with a girl in a blue-and-gold practice jersey with "Holland Middle School" printed on the front. Peyton walked over towards the coach and stopped just a few feet away.

Coach Anderson saw Peyton and immediately waved her closer. "Nice to see you, Peyton," coach said. "There are practice jerseys in a box in the corner. Grab one and get changed in the locker room." She pointed to a door on the far end of the gymnasium. "Practice begins in about five minutes."

Peyton searched the box and found a jersey with an *S* on the tag, grabbed it, and jogged to the locker room. Entering, she noticed seven other girls who had either already changed into their practice gear or were close to being finished.

One of the girls, a tall, skinny redhead barked out, "Who are you, and what are you doing here?"

"My name is Peyton, and I'm trying out for the team."

"I've never seen you before. Do you even go to school here?" demanded another girl.

"Uh . . . well, no, I don't," Peyton replied shyly. "I go to Holland Elementary."

"What do you mean?" snapped a short blonde girl standing against one of the lockers.

"Well, I am in fourth grade at Holland Elementary School," Peyton replied.

All seven girls in the room looked at each other and laughed. The tall red-headed girl looked right at Peyton and whispered in a low voice, "This is the middle school basketball tryout. I think you're in the wrong place."

Peyton looked back at all the girls and with hesitation said, "Coach Anderson asked me to try out."

The locker room went silent while all seven girls looked back and forth at each other and at Peyton.

"What a joke," said the short blonde as she walked past Peyton and out the door toward the gym.

"I don't know what's up, but I'll tell you this. I was the captain last year, and I plan on being the captain again this year, and I don't like this one bit," said the tall redhead as she passed Peyton, giving her a little shoulder bump on the way out the locker-room door.

All five other girls followed the redhead out the door, leaving Peyton in the locker room by herself. *Wow*, Peyton thought to herself, *that didn't go very well*. She got changed, laced up her sneakers, and headed out the door into the gym.

CHAPTER 4

"Balls on the ball rack and everyone on the baseline!" Coach Anderson yelled while blowing the whistle hanging around her neck. All sixteen girls in practice attire returned the basketballs to the ball rack and lined up on the baseline.

Once all the girls were all in place, Coach Anderson announced, "Welcome to the Holland Middle School basketball tryouts. I am Coach Anderson, and this is Coach Havers."

Coach Havers stood about six feet three, with blonde hair and a ponytail. She looked like a professional basketball player in her Adidas sweat suit and high-top basketball sneakers.

"You will have the next three days to show Coach Havers and me you belong on this team," Coach continued. "We plan on keeping thirteen girls, so that means three of you will not make the team. I'm not interested what you've done in the past or how good you think you may be. I will make the final decision, and no one is guaranteed anything."

Peyton immediately liked Coach Anderson and was encouraged that she was going to give everyone a fair chance. Practice began like any other practice Peyton had ever attended: stretching, a short jog around the gym, and layup lines. After about fifteen minutes of the typical warm-up activities, practice suddenly took a much different approach.

"Forwards and centers at the far end of the gym with Coach Havers, and guards stay here with me," Coach Anderson announced.

Peyton had never played on a team with more than one coach, so the fact that the players were being split up to work with different coaches based on the position they played was new to her. Peyton stayed at the end with Coach Anderson. Peyton had played point guard her entire life. Along with Peyton, seven other girls stayed with Coach Anderson. Peyton took a look at her competition. On a basketball team, the shorter players usually played point guard or shooting guard. That meant that there were approximately four girls for each position. Peyton also noticed that she was by far the smallest girl in the group. Being a fourth grader, it made sense, since all the other girls were either in seventh or eighth grade.

Coach Anderson set cones out across the gymnasium in a straight line about four feet apart.

"Alright, listen up. I want you to dribble between the cones using your left and right hands. Once you get to the last cone, sprint in a straight line, continuing to dribble back to the first cone!" Coach Anderson yelled. "Line up and let's get going!"

Peyton hurried to the front of the line and waited for the coach to blow her whistle.

Bleep! Peyton took off dribbling, weaving in and out of cones. When she arrived at the last cone, she turned and continued to dribble, sprinting as fast as she could to where Coach Anderson was standing. She noticed that when she passed the final cone, Coach Anderson pressed a button on a stopwatch and wrote a number in a notebook she was holding. Peyton waited until the other seven girls had finished, watching each with curious anticipation, wondering if she was quicker than the others.

Coach Anderson proceeded to run the girls through additional dribbling drills, shooting drills, and passing drills, all the time writing numbers and notes in her notebook. During these drills, it became obvious to Peyton that one of the girls

12

in her group was by far the best player among the guards. This girl, who was wearing a black headband, appeared to be about five feet tall, and she was fast and strong, and it seemed as if she never missed a shot. Peyton didn't know her name, but coach kept referring to her as "Sheed."

While Peyton's group was participating in these drills, Coach Havers's group was also performing a variety of drills while she also wrote numbers and notes in her notebook.

After two intense hours of practice, Coach Anderson blew the whistle for the final time that day and told the girls that practice was over and to be back at the same time tomorrow. All the girls were dripping with sweat and slowly walked toward the drinking fountain and locker room. Everyone seemed tired and drained. Peyton had never been through a more difficult and demanding practice in her life.

Sitting in the locker room after practice, Peyton began glancing around trying to gauge whether or not everyone else was as tired as she was. All sixteen girls seemed equally drained, but after a few moments, the girls began talking amongst themselves, and Peyton noticed a few looking her way while whispering and giving dirty looks. Peyton decided that it would be in her best interest to get changed and leave as soon as possible. As she was packing her sneakers in her gym bag, the girl in with the black headband walked over to her.

"Hey. I don't know your name, but you did good today."

As the girl in the black headband was beginning to turn and walk away, Peyton replied, "My name is Peyton, and thanks." The girl coach had referred to as Sheed acknowledged her with a smile and walked away.

When Peyton left the middle school, she could see her father's car parked next to the sidewalk. She opened the car door, threw her gym bag and backpack in the backseat, and sat down.

"Well, how was it?" Dad asked.

"I think I did alright, but I'm not sure. The girls are really good, Dad, and they are all bigger than I am," Peyton replied. "I have never been through such a tough practice in my life. Coach Anderson split us into two groups. The guards were with her, and the forwards and centers were with Coach Havers. Coach Havers is the assistant coach. I'm exhausted, Dad."

"Well, honey, we'll get you home, and you can take a shower and we'll have some dinner," Dad said quietly.

At dinner, Peyton answered all the questions her mother and father had for her, being careful not to mention the treatment she had received from the other girls on the team. The last thing she needed was for her parents to get worried and question whether or not she should even be trying out.

By the time dinner was over and she had finished her homework, she was absolutely exhausted. Peyton headed to bed around eight thirty and lay in bed staring at the ceiling. She couldn't help thinking about the day's practice. The girls on the middle school basketball team were better than she thought. She was used to being the best player on the team, but now she wasn't. She couldn't help but wonder if she stood out to the coaches. Was she better than some of the other girls? Would she make the team?

CHAPTER 5

Peyton had no idea when she fell asleep, but she woke to her alarm beeping at the side of her bed. The moment she woke, Peyton could feel the throbbing ache in her legs. She had never felt this pain before, but then she had never been through a practice as difficult as yesterday's either. By the time she had taken a shower and made her way down the stairs, the soreness had begun to subside.

"Good morning, dear," Mom said in her usually cheerful voice while placing a bowl of cereal in front of Peyton. "How are you doing this morning?"

"My legs are pretty achy, but I'm feeling okay." Peyton looked at her father, who had just finished pouring himself a cup of coffee. "Dad, what if I don't make the team?"

"If you don't, you don't. It's not the end of the world, dear. Just do your best and I'm sure everything will work out."

Peyton finished her breakfast, grabbed her backpack and gym bag, and headed out the door to school. On her way, she couldn't help but think about practice, the girls on the team, and her performance from the day before.

After another long day of school, Peyton headed back to the middle school for practice. The next two days at practice were similar to the first. The girls were split up, and Coach Anderson and Coach Havers worked with their groups of girls. They participated in all sorts of drills and competitions under close supervision from the coaches. At the end of practice on the third day, Coach Anderson asked all the girls to sit down at center court.

"Alright, listen up. Thank you for coming out for the team. I wish I could keep all of you, but I only have thirteen jerseys. Coach Havers and I have been watching you these last three days and we need to make some decisions. We will make cuts and post the team list on the bulletin board outside the girls' locker room tomorrow. Any questions? If there are no questions, I will see all of you who made the team tomorrow for practice at three thirty here in the gym."

Coach Anderson and Coach Havers walked away, leaving all the girls sitting in the middle of the gymnasium. Peyton, along with the other girls, slowly got up and began walking toward the locker room. No one really said much while in the locker room, and Peyton hurriedly gathered her stuff and walked out.

In the car ride home, she didn't say much. She just stared out the window and thought to herself. Dad interrupted the silence.

"Don't worry about making the team, Peyton. As long as you've given your best effort, then that's all you can do."

Peyton looked at her father, nodded in agreement, and then stared back out the window for the remainder of the ride home. She knew she had given her best effort, but was that enough?

Peyton was physically and mentally tired, and she made it through dinner without saying much. Thank goodness her parents didn't bombard her with a million questions about practice. After dinner, she made her way upstairs and began working on her math homework, but she couldn't concentrate. All she could think about was whether or not she made the team. She decided that she would wake up early and go to the middle school to check the list. There was no way she could sit through an entire day of school knowing that a list on the bulletin board outside the girls' locker room either contained her name or didn't. She had to know first thing in the morning.

While working on her math Peyton heard the phone ring. She didn't think anything of it and knew her mom or dad would answer it. A few minutes later, she heard her father call her from the bottom of the stairs, "Peyton, could you please come down here? Mom and I need to talk to you."

Peyton placed her pencil in her math book and closed it. She headed downstairs and into the kitchen where her mom and dad were sitting at the table.

"Sit down, sweetie," said Dad. "Coach Anderson just called."

Peyton's eyes immediately fixed on her father's.

"What did she want?" Peyton asked, not knowing if she really wanted to hear the answer.

"You made the team, dear."

Peyton leapt up in the air. "Are you serious? Did I really make it?"

"Yes, you really made it!" Dad answered back.

Peyton hugged her mom and dad and ran into the living room and jumped on the couch.

"Coach knew that since you aren't in the middle school, that it would be best if she called so you didn't worry about it," her father said, but Peyton barely heard him. Her mind was racing, and all she could think about was the fact that she made the Holland Middle School girls' basketball team.

CHAPTER 6

Peyton walked into basketball practice the next day with nervous anticipation. She knew that many of the girls did not like her, but she didn't care. She was going to make the best of her situation and play basketball.

After getting changed, Peyton found herself shooting baskets waiting for practice to officially begin. None of the girls around her spoke to her. They laughed and talked amongst themselves. Peyton could hear a lot of their conversations, and most of it revolved around boys or teachers in the middle school. While she was shooting practice free throws, she noticed out of the corner of her eye the girl the coaches referred to as Sheed walking towards her.

"Hey," said the girl, "my name is Rasheeda. People call me Sheed for short. I know a lot of the girls on the team have a problem with you because you're a fourth grader. I'm not one of them. I want to win, and if you're good enough to help us win, that's all that matters to me."

Peyton was caught off guard by Rasheeda's comment and could only mutter a simple "Uh, okay."

Just then the whistle blew and the first day of middle school basketball practice began. Practice was much different from tryouts. Coach Anderson and Coach Havers immediately began teaching the girls specific offensive plays that would be implemented against opponents during games. All the girls on the team were given positions and expected to remember where on the court they were supposed to be during a set play call. Peyton immediately found herself at the point guard position, which is where she had played her entire life, but as practice proceeded, she noticed that the team was divided into two groups, the blue group and gold group.

Every girl had a reversible practice jersey with a blue and gold side. The first group was comprised of five girls, and these girls were asked to wear the blue side. That five included the tall redhead, Joellel, who had given her attitude in the locker room the first day of tryouts, the short blonde named Addison, who had also spoke with her in the locker room, and Rasheeda. The group also included another tall husky girl named Emily, and another short, skinny girl named Sasha. It became obvious very quickly that these five girls were going to be the first team. The first team, or starters, consisted of the players that always began the basketball game and usually played the majority of minutes. Peyton had always been one of the starters ever since she began playing basketball. Although it had occurred to her that she might not start, it bothered her that she had already been relegated to the second team, the backups.

The second Peyton sat down in the car seat, her father knew something was wrong.

"How was the first day of practice?"

"Coach has me on the second team already," Peyton replied, wiping a tear from her eye.

"Peyton, you're not always going to be the best player, and you're not going to start on every basketball team you play on," her father said with an abruptness she was unfamiliar with. "If you're not happy with being on the second team, then figure out what it is you need to do to fix it. Use the fact that you're on the second team to motivate you to work hard and improve!"

Peyton and her father remained silent the remainder of the car ride home. After entering the house, Peyton immediately dropped her backpack and gym bag on the mudroom floor and headed upstairs. She sat in her room and stared at the trophies and awards scattered around. Sitting on her bed, Peyton began thinking about practice, the girls on the team, being on the second team, and what her father had said in the car. It wasn't long before she realized that her father was right. She wasn't going to be the starter, and she had to deal with that. She could either sulk about it or work harder. At that moment, she decided that she was going to work hard.

Peyton returned to practice the next day with a new perspective. She had come to grips with her role on the team, and she was going to make the best of it. As the team continued learning new plays and practicing them, Peyton made a point of working as hard or harder than anyone else. She was determined to make the coaches see that she deserved to play.

Peyton was the point guard on the second team, or gold group, which meant that she was constantly in opposition to the point guard on the first team, which was Addison. Addison was a very good ball handler, but she didn't pass the ball often, and her jump shot was only mediocre. Peyton felt that her ball handling was just as good as Addison's, that she was much quicker, and she felt she had a better jump shot as well. The biggest difference between the two was that Addison was in eighth grade, had playing experience from the previous year, and she was about four feet eight inches tall, four inches taller than Peyton, and Peyton had no middle school playing experience. Peyton knew there was no way to overcome the height differential, but if she worked hard enough, she could prove to the coaches that her talent and skills were just as good if not better than Addison's. *I may not be the starter, but hopefully I will be able to earn playing time*, Peyton thought to herself.

As the days and practices proceeded. Peyton remained a fixture on the second team. The first game was in three weeks, and Peyton knew that was the amount of time she had to impress the coaches. She continued to work hard and give a hundred percent.

As practice after practice went by, players on the team began talking more and more with Peyton. Her second-team teammates asked questions about specific plays and congratulated her when they succeeded as a unit. Peyton also became more vocal. She knew as a point guard and the floor leader, she had to have constant communication with her teammates. She encouraged and congratulated them, and little by little she began earning their trust.

Peyton also noticed over this period of time that Addison wasn't very well liked by the other girls on the team. She had one really good friend: the redhead named Joellel. The other girls on the team argued and confronted her quite often. Many of the confrontations were based on the issue that Addison was a ball hog. As a point guard, you have the basketball in your possession more than any other player on the team, and it is your responsibility to get the ball to your teammates in situations that make them and the team successful. Addison didn't do this. She often kept the ball in her possession too much and took unadvised shots. When players on the team questioned her about her decision-making, she often remarked with unpleasant tones or glaring stares. Peyton even noticed Coach Anderson and Coach Havers often talking with Addison about her decision-making.

Another player Peyton noticed arguing with Addison quite often was Rasheeda. It was clear to Peyton and everyone on the team that Rasheeda was by far the most talented player. She was the shooting guard and the leading scorer from last year's team.

She had a great jump shot and could score against anyone. Many of the plays Coach Anderson had created were intended to get Rasheeda the basketball in positions to score. The problem was that the plays had to be executed, and that began with Addison. Peyton had played enough basketball in her life to know that with Addison leading this basketball team, the plays were not going to be executed properly, and that meant that the team was in for a very long year.

CHAPTER 7

Three days before Holland Middle School's first basketball game, Coach Anderson blew her whistle and ended practice fifteen minutes early.

"Everyone sit at mid court. Coach Havers and I are passing out paper and pencils. We are asking you to list your top two choices for team captain. Prior to making your decision, you need to think about the characteristics that a captain should possess. I don't expect you to choose your best friend or the most popular girl on the team. I expect you to choose the individuals who will provide the greatest amount of leadership. All votes will be kept confidential."

As Peyton glanced around at the girls sitting in the center of the gym, she contemplated whom she was going to choose. Rasheeda was definitely going to get her vote, but who else? Peyton finally decided to vote for Joellel. Joellel had given her attitude and been unfriendly from the moment Peyton met her, but she was a very good basketball player, and she was outspoken and not afraid to challenge anyone on the team. After handing in her votes, Peyton headed to the locker room and changed.

While she was leaving the locker room and heading toward the door leading out of the gymnasium, she heard a voice from behind, "Peyton! Wait up!"

As Peyton turned toward the voice, she noticed Rasheeda jogging to catch up with her.

"Hey. I just wanted to let you know that I chose you as one of the team captains." Peyton was shocked—not only at the fact that Rasheeda chose her, but also that she told her.

"I know you're in fourth grade, but I've seen more leadership out of you than most other girls on this team," Rasheeda continued. "Like I told you before, I don't care about your age or anything else. You can help us win, and I want to win. I don't want to repeat last year's record."

Peyton, who was caught off guard, could only mumble a "thanks" in return before Rasheeda turned and walked out of the gym.

Holland Middle School was scheduled to play eight games over the course of the season. The league Holland participated in consisted of ten teams spread out over the county. At the end of the regular season, eight of the ten teams made the playoffs. Holland Middle School finished in ninth place the previous year. This year, their first game was scheduled against Brookfield Middle School. Brookfield was the defending champion and had a reputation for being the best team in the league year after year.

At practice the day before the game, Coach Anderson announced to the team that Rasheeda and Joellel had been chosen team captains, and as captains they were the two "coaches" on the basketball court.

Practices the day before games were much different than normal practices. The girls participated in simple shooting drills, discussed offensive and defensive strategies, and practiced walk-throughs. Walk-throughs are when the players practice the designed plays that they are going to use the following day during the game. The practices are intended to be easier so as not to wear out the players before a game.

That day, while Coach Havers worked with the girls, Coach Anderson asked each girl, one by one, to talk with her at the far end of the gymnasium away from the ears of the rest of the girls. Along with Coach Anderson, Rasheeda and Joellel were also present. Peyton did not know what to expect when her name was called, so she headed in Coach Anderson's direction a little nervously.

"Hello, Peyton. I just wanted to give you an understanding of what Coach Havers and I feel will be your role on the team this year."

Peyton stood quietly, anticipating Coach's next few words.

"As of right now, you are the back up to Addison at the point guard position. Addison will play the majority of the minutes, but you will also play some. You need to be mentally ready at all times during the game, because you never know when your name might be called to replace her. I know that you are used to playing the entire game, so this will be an adjustment for you. Do you think you can handle your role on this team?"

Peyton looked at Rasheeda and Joellel and then back at coach. "Yes," she muttered.

"Okay, good. Do you have any questions?" Coach Anderson asked.

Peyton shook her head, and Coach dismissed her back to practice. As Peyton walked away, she was disappointed but not surprised. She had been Addison's backup for the last three weeks, and she had expected to be the backup once the season began.

CHAPTER 8

Finally it was the day of the first game of the year. After another long day at school filled with waiting and anticipation for the big game, the last bell rang, signaling the end of the school day. Peyton rushed over to the middle school to begin preparation for the game. Although she wasn't starting, Peyton was still very nervous. She was always nervous prior to a game, but this was different. She felt as if she was going to throw up. She wasn't starting, but she knew that she had to be ready at all times because coach could call on her to enter the game at any time. As the team participated in pre-game warm-ups Peyton felt her nervousness and anxiety ease. Her jump shot felt good, and she was ready if needed.

The game began, and Brookfield Middle School jumped out to a big lead. Brookfield appeared to be a well-oiled machine, and they outscored Holland 18-6 in the first quarter behind their superstar point guard, Katy Spinelli. Katy was the league's most valuable player from the previous year.

During the first quarter break, Coach Anderson reminded the girls to stick to the game plan and run the plays like they had practiced. Coach looked directly at Addison and pleaded with her to get the ball to the players in a position to score. It wasn't until four minutes remained in the second quarter before the coach finally called Peyton's name.

"Peyton! Go give Addison a breather!"

Peyton ran to the scorer's table and waited patiently for the next dead ball and her chance to enter the game. After a foul on Rasheeda, Peyton was able to enter the game. After Brookfield made two more points at the free throw line, the ball was inbounded to Peyton, and she began dribbling up court. With the score 24-10, Peyton knew that she had to get the ball to Joellel and Rasheeda if there was any chance of making a comeback.

After crossing mid court, Peyton heard coach yelling from the sideline, "Run the flex! Run the flex!"

Peyton yelled out "Flex!" to her teammates and immediately passed the ball to Sasha and ran to the opposite side of the court to set a pick on Rasheeda's defender. As Peyton stood to set the pick, she felt Rasheeda's defender elbow her in the neck while trying to get past. Although the pain was excruciating, Peyton held her ground, and Rasheeda freed herself from her defender for a split second. Sasha passed the ball to Rasheeda, and Rasheeda shot the ball and scored the basket. Still in pain from the elbow to the neck, Peyton ran back down court to get set up on defense.

When she passed Coach Anderson and the Holland bench, she heard coach complimenting her. "Great pick, Peyton! Way to hold your ground!"

Peyton acknowledged coach with a head nod and focused back on her opponent, waiting to play defense. Peyton had few opportunities to make another impact on her team and coaches in the next few minutes and was replaced by Addison a short time later. Addison also proved to be ineffective against the Brookfield defense, and by the end of the game the final score was Brookfield 45, Holland 27. Peyton had played six out of a total of thirty-two minutes.

The team sat in the locker room after the game, heads down, dejected and disappointed. Brookfield had beaten them handily in every aspect of the game from the opening tip-off. It had never been close. After the game, in the locker room, Coach addressed the team, said a few words of encouragement and informed them about the next day's practice schedule.

As Peyton was getting changed, she couldn't help but overhear Emily and Sasha talking about the game. She wasn't able to make out everything that was being said, but she was able to get the overall message of the conversation: they were complaining about Addison.

CHAPTER 9

Peyton was surprised to find her mother, and especially her father, so upbeat and proud of the way she played.

"Great game, honey," her mom insisted.

"You were outstanding out there!" Dad said.

With a look of bewilderment, Peyton responded with shock and wonderment, "Why are you congratulating me? We lost. Matter of fact, we got rocked."

Dad was the first to fire back. "Are you kidding me? You don't give yourself enough credit. You just played against middle school girls, and you played well. You should be proud of yourself. Yes, you lost as a team, and that is never a good thing, but you contributed to your team, and that's what you need to feel proud about!"

Even though Peyton knew her dad was correct in everything he'd said, she couldn't help but feel disappointed. She was used to winning or at least being competitive. Today, for the first time in her basketball career, she felt embarrassed by the way her team performed.

That night while lying in bed, Peyton recalled her involvement in the game. What could she have done differently? Did she make the right decisions while relieving Addison? Then her mind drifted to Addison and the conversation she overheard after the game. Were other girls on the team frustrated with Addison, and if so, what did that mean for the team as a whole?

What did that mean for her? That was Peyton's last thought as she quickly faded into sleep.

The next day at practice, Coach talked briefly to the team about the loss to Brookfield, and then began talking about the upcoming game against Jefferson Middle School. The Jefferson game was in a few days, and it was apparent that the team still needed a lot of work on offense. Against Brookfield, the offense never really got going and the plays were not run according to plan, so that day the team worked entirely on executing the offensive plays over and over.

Throughout practice, Coach Anderson consistently barked out commands and stopped the practice if a play was not run correctly. Often, the one individual that the coach had to speak to was Addison. Time and time again, Addison was in the wrong position, attempted an ill-advised pass, or took an inappropriate shot. Peyton noticed her coach's frustration, and it was obvious to the players on the team that Addison became more upset and defiant every time Coach stopped practice to talk with her.

After practice, while Peyton was walking towards the gymnasium door preparing to meet her father, she felt a tap on her shoulder. Turning around, Peyton noticed it had been Rasheeda who tapped her.

"Hey, what's up? Peyton asked.

"Just wanted to know if you are interested in coming to my house Saturday and shooting some hoops."

"Um, this Saturday? Yeah, I think I can. Let me talk with my parents and I'll let you know tomorrow."

When Peyton got in her father's car, she immediately asked if there were any plans for the weekend. When dad replied no, Peyton asked if she could go to Rasheeda's house on Saturday to practice shooting.

"I don't see why not, but we'll double check with Mom, and if you can get her parents phone number, I'll give her a call just to double-check that it's alright." Peyton smiled the remainder of the car ride home.

Mom had no objection to Peyton spending Saturday at Rasheeda's house, so at practice the next day, Peyton told Rasheeda that she would come over. Rasheeda told her to be over around one p.m.

Rasheeda lived just outside town, and when Peyton arrived at her house, Rasheeda met her in the driveway.

"Hi Peyton," Rasheeda called, walking towards the car.

Peyton got out of the car, waved goodbye to her mother, and walked over to Rasheeda. "Thanks again for having me over. I don't see a hoop in your driveway. Do you have a park nearby where we can play?"

Rasheeda just looked at Peyton and said, "Follow me."

Rasheeda led Peyton around the back of her house and stopped. Peyton's mouth hung open, and she just stared. She stood staring at an incredible basketball court that Rasheeda had in her backyard. It was a full court equipped with painted end lines, free throw lines, and three-point lines. There were adjustable basketball hoops at both ends, and it even had lights!

"Are you kidding me?" Peyton gasped. "How did you get this? This is unbelievable!"

"My dad owns a concrete business and poured the concrete himself. Then we just got the hoops, painted the lines, and installed a few lights with the help of my uncle."

Peyton couldn't believe it. It was nicer than most parks in town. "You're so lucky to have this!"

"I know," Rasheeda responded. "My dad and I practice a lot back here. This is where I spend most of my free time."

After Peyton's initial shock wore off, the girls spent the next few hours shooting, dribbling, and working on various drills.

Taking a water break, Rasheeda started talking about the team. "I hate to say it, but I don't think we're going to win very many games this year. Addison is killing us. She hurt us last year, and nothing's changed. I thought that with new coaches there might be a chance that things would be different. I know you're the backup and in fourth grade, but you're better, Peyton. No doubt. You are better than Addison."

"I think so too," Peyton responded without hesitation. "I think that Addison has all the athletic skills to be a great point guard, but she is selfish. She wants to do her own thing, and she doesn't run the plays the way they are supposed to be run."

"I don't know what's going to happen, but like I told you before, I want to win," Rasheeda said with determination.

After a few more hours of shooting, dribbling, and talking, Peyton's father pulled into the driveway to pick up his daughter. On the way home, Peyton told him all about Rasheeda's basketball court and their conversation about the team, all the while beaming with happiness. Not only had Peyton been able to spend an incredible day playing basketball, but she felt that she had also become much closer with Rasheeda.

CHAPTER 10

Although Jefferson Middle School was not nearly as good as Brookfield, the game was not close. Like the Brookfield game, Jefferson jumped out to an early first quarter lead, and Holland was never able to get it closer than ten points. The final score was Jefferson 52, Holland 38.

Similar to the first game, Addison played the majority of the minutes, scoring ten points, but she only contributed three assists and was responsible for seven turnovers. Peyton played seven total minutes. She scored only three points, but she had five assists and committed only one turnover. Rasheeda led all scorers with fourteen points, while Joellel contributed eight.

After the game, the locker room was full of tension and unhappiness. Peyton could feel the uneasiness, and there was an atmosphere of frustration. Coach Anderson and Coach Havers were not pleased with the team, and it was evident.

"This is not the kind of basketball that Coach and I expect from this team," Coach Anderson began. "We are better than this! We look as if we haven't practiced together all year long. We're not moving the ball on offense; we're not talking with each other on defense. We need to refocus and get back to basics. Be ready for a hard practice tomorrow. We'll get this right one way or another!"

With that, the two coaches moved to the far end of the locker room and began conferencing with each other. After the coaches had vacated the immediate area where the girls were sitting, grumbling began. Peyton heard Addison mumble something to Joellel and shoot a look at Rasheeda. Joellel looked back at Addison and walked away. Peyton didn't know what Addison said or why Joellel walked away, but she knew that there was discontent on the team. Holland Middle had just completed its second game and their record was 0-2. There were six games left, and the team was already at the bottom of the league standings. The problem was that if the team didn't get on the same page quickly, there would be no playoffs for a second consecutive year.

The next day at practice was the most demanding of the year. Coach was still obviously upset, and from Peyton's viewpoint, she took it out on the team. Once again, the entire practice was dedicated to working on the offense. Every time someone was in the wrong position, the coach made the team run leg burners. Leg burners are designed to get a basketball team in shape. To complete a leg burner, every player has to line up on the baseline, run and touch the foul line closest to the end line, then run back and touch the end line, then run and touch the half court line, run back and touch the end line, run and touch the opposite foul line, run back and touch the end line, and finally run and touch the opposite end line before running back to finish at the end line that you started from. They are absolutely exhausting. From Peyton's estimate, the team probably ran ten of those during practice.

When Coach finally blew the whistle officially ending practice, the entire team fell to the gymnasium floor, gasping for air.

"This was not meant as a punishment," Coach began. "You need to understand that in order to be successful as a team, it's imperative that you do exactly what I ask. When I instruct you to run a specific play, I expect it to be run. When I yell out a specific

34

defense, I expect you to listen. We will be successful if, and only if, we as a team play as a team, not as individuals. Today, you learned that when you play as individuals you suffer. Hopefully, we suffer here at practice rather than in our next game! See you tomorrow. Same time!" Coach Anderson gave one last look at her team lying on the floor and walked away.

As the girls slowly started sitting up and moving, Rasheeda was the first to speak up. "We need to listen to Coach and play as a team. Two games so far, and we haven't been close yet. I want to make the playoffs, and we only have six games left. Let's all get on the same page and work together."

Looking around at the faces of the girls sitting on the gym floor, Peyton noticed all the girls looking at Rasheeda and nodding in agreement, with one exception, Addison.

CHAPTER 11

Game three was scheduled against Eastside Middle School. Eastside's record was also 0-2, and they had struggled to score points in both games they played that season. They lost the first game 62-24, and the second game 45-18. Everyone on the Holland Middle School team knew that they had to win this game. A day before the game, spirits were high, and the girls felt better about the way practice had gone ever since coach's last speech about teamwork.

During their customary walk-through practice, Coach Anderson pulled Peyton aside to talk. "Peyton, Coach Havers and I have been talking, and we are very pleased with the progress we've seen from you in such a short period of time. I know you're unhappy with the amount of playing time you're receiving. However, you need to continue to work hard and push Addison in practice. You'll get your chance in games as the season progresses."

Peyton looked at coach and nodded, letting her know that she understood what was being asked of her. Peyton returned to practice not quite sure of what to make of the coach's comments. Did she need to work harder? Was she only being used to challenge Addison? Or were the coaches preparing her for a larger role on the team? Maybe they saw in Addison what Peyton saw in Addison. Either way, Peyton decided that she needed to continue to work hard, improve, and be ready.

During the first quarter against Eastside, Holland quickly jumped out to an early eight-point lead, and by the end of the quarter they led 18-6. For the first time this season, the team was actually playing as a cohesive group. Players were in the right places on offense, and the team was also playing well on defense. During the first quarter intermission, Coach Anderson continued to preach the importance of teamwork and efficiency.

The second quarter began, and that's when the team began falling apart. Everything they had done well in the first quarter immediately disappeared. Players weren't in the right places, there wasn't any communication, and Addison began taking ill-advised shots. The score quickly changed from 18-6 to 18-18. By halftime, Holland was trailing 24-22.

During the halftime speech, Coach continued to stress ball movement, teamwork, and communication. Peyton sat in her locker staring blankly at her coach. She was listening but at the same time wondering if she would get a chance to play. She had not seen a minute of floor time in the first half, and she knew that if given the chance she could help this team win. The third quarter started the way the second quarter ended. Addison quickly began deviating from the called plays, forcing poor shots and turning the ball over to the other team. Eastside took the lead and slowly began extending the margin, and by the end of the third quarter the score was 38-29 in Eastside's favor.

At the quarter intermission, Peyton heard coach call her name. "Peyton, go give Addison a breather."

Peyton, surprised to hear her name, quickly raced to the scorer's table to be recognized so she could enter the game. When play began, Peyton immediately took the inbounds from Emily and started dribbling up court.

"Flex, run flex!" Peyton shouted.

She dribbled to the right side of the court and passed the ball to a slashing Sasha. Peyton then hustled to the opposite side of the floor, where she set a pick on Joellel's defender. Joellel moved around the pick, and Sasha gave Joellel a perfect bounce pass. Joellel grabbed the ball, took one step, and laid the ball in the basket. Peyton slapped five to Joellel, and she and her teammates quickly hustled back down the floor to set up on defense.

As Eastside's point guard, who was wearing jersey number five, dribbled up the court, Peyton watched closely and noticed that she was dribbling the ball out in front of her body. Peyton knew that if she timed her move, she could easily take the ball away. She waited for the right moment, and then when she saw her opportunity, she swiped her hand down towards the ball and knocked it away from her opponent. Peyton pounced on the ball and raced down court with Eastside's point guard close behind. She stretched her hands out and laid the ball off the backboard just as the defender slapped her arm.

Bleep! The referee blew the whistle and made the hand motion for a good basket plus a free throw. The basket counted and Peyton was headed to the free throw line for one foul shot. Rasheeda and Joellel raced down and congratulated Peyton with a series of high fives and shouts after the great play.

Peyton collected herself and stepped to the free throw line. She bent her knees and snapped her wrist. *Swish.* The ball fell through the net, and Peyton and her team headed back down court to set up on defense. The score now stood at 38-34, and with five straight points Holland seemed to have a new sense of enthusiasm.

Eastside's point guard slowly began to dribble up court, and once again Peyton waited patiently on the opposite side of half court. Starring at her opponent, Peyton noticed a new expression on her face. She recognized this expression from so many of the girls she had played against in leagues and tournaments—fear! The opposing point guard was scared, and her eyes gave her away. It was obvious that the last possession had rattled her. Peyton knew that this was her chance and immediately leaped towards the nervous point guard with hands waving. The Eastside point guard panicked and attempted a pass to a teammate on the wing. The teammate was not in position and the ball sailed out of bounds. Peyton could hear her coach and many of her teammates on the bench yelling praises and encouragement.

After taking the ball inbounds, Peyton hurried down court and called out "Post!" Emily and Joellel ran to the two elbows, while Rasheeda and Sasha positioned themselves on the blocks.

"Post, post!" Peyton called out again.

Emily and Joellel sprinted to the blocks and set picks on Rasheeda and Sasha's defenders. Peyton dribbled to Rasheeda's side and waited for her to sprint around from Joellel's pick. Peyton rocketed the ball at Rasheeda's chest. Rasheeda grabbed the ball and faced the basket. After setting the pick for Rasheeda, Joellel sealed her defender and positioned herself to receive the ball. Rasheeda bounced the ball to Joellel in the post, and Joellel turned and shot a jump hook over her defender. The ball bounced off the glass and sank through the hoop. The score was tie, and Eastside called a timeout.

As Peyton and her teammates headed to their bench, they were met with high fives and congratulations. Coach calmed the team down and began explaining the offensive and defensive strategies for the remainder of the game.

"Here's what we're going to do. I want to full court press them. Peyton has rattled their point guard, and now is our chance to exploit Eastside's weakness. Rasheeda, you guard the inbound pass, and as soon as the ball is passed inbounds, you go and double-team the first person to get it. Peyton, you rotate to

Rasheeda's previous man and look for the steal. Let's put them away!"

The team left the huddle with energy and enthusiasm. The Holland girls positioned themselves like coach asked and waited for Eastside to take the ball out of bounds. The moment the Eastside player inbounded the ball, Rasheeda leapt towards the player receiving the ball to set up the double-team. Peyton slid into position, and when the Eastside player attempted the backward pass, Peyton intercepted it, gathered herself, and shot the ball towards the rim. The ball rolled around the rim and fell through the net. For the first time since the beginning of the second quarter, Holland had the lead.

For the remainder of the game, Holland pressured Eastside on defense, and with Peyton running the point guard position, they continued to get good shots on offense. Holland pulled away and won the game 52-40.

In the locker room after the game, the girls were ecstatic. Everyone was slapping high fives, congratulating each other and enjoying the moment—everyone except Addison. Addison was by her locker untying her shoes and glaring at Peyton. While the team continued celebrating and enjoying themselves, Addison quietly changed and left the locker room.

CHAPTER 12

Peyton's parents continued the celebration when their daughter arrived home.

"Awesome game!" said her father, slapping her high five. "You guys were amazing out there. You fought back and really played as a team. And you, sweetie, were the reason!"

Peyton's smile was as bright as sunshine. She knew she was a big reason they won the game. For the first time since joining the middle school basketball team, Peyton felt that she genuinely helped the team.

The next day at practice, Peyton was surprised to find herself still on the second team. She was confused. The team struggled with Addison in the game. The team played well when she was in, so why was she still on the second team? Although confused and frustrated, Peyton knew that she couldn't dwell on the fact that she was still a second-team member. Last night's game proved she was cape able of contributing and being a productive player for the team. *Practice hard and practice smart,* she told herself. *Everything will work itself out.*

From the moment practice began, she noticed the agitation and irritation emulating from Addison. The surprising thing was that Addison wasn't only taking her frustration out on Peyton, which Peyton expected, but she was taking it out on everyone, players and coaches. Addison began the practice arguing with Coach Havers during a simple shooting drill in which the coach had instructed Addison to use the backboard when shooting from the side perimeter. Addison immediately fired back, "That's not how I like to shoot from the wing!"

In the next drill, Addison barked at Sasha for not outletting the ball to her in a timely manner after Sasha rebounded the ball. Sasha responded with a "too bad." The most surprising confrontation took place while the team was participating in fine-tuning some of their offensive plays. While running the play fist, Addison passed the ball to the wing to Rasheeda. Addison then went to the opposite side of the floor to set a pick on Joellel's defender. Joellel curled around the pick and received the pass from Rasheeda. Addison then faked one way and then cut backdoor toward the basket. Joellel attempted a bounce pass, but the pass bounced at Addison's feet and trickled out of bounds.

"Are you kidding me?" Addison screamed. "That pass sucked!"

Joellel looked at Addison with bewilderment. Joellel was Addison's only real friend left on the team. Addison's attitude had alienated her from everyone else, and now it seemed that she was criticizing her last and only supporter.

"Hey! That's enough!" yelled an irate Coach Anderson. "That is not how we treat our teammates. You're done for the day! Hit the showers!" Coach Anderson pointed at the locker room while glaring at Addison.

Addison, in a last sign of defiance, threw the basketball to the opposite end of the court and began walking toward the locker room.

"You'll go get that ball if you know what's good for you," replied Coach Anderson in a very cool and calm voice. Addison continued walking toward the locker room, ignoring Coach's warning. All of the Holland Middle School girls stood silent and staring, not believing what they just witnessed.

Bleep!

"Alright, Peyton, fill in and run fist again," Coach announced.

The players took their positions and ran the play as they were told. For the remainder of practice the team was uncharacteristically quiet. That day after practice, unbeknownst to Peyton, the two captains, Rasheeda and Joellel, sat with Coach Anderson and Coach Havers.

"Coach," began Rasheeda, "Joellel and I have talked, and we feel that Peyton gives us the best shot at winning, and we are asking you to start her over Addison. Peyton is a team player and Addison isn't. As captains, we feel this is best for the team." Coach thanked the girls and told them that captains sometimes have to make difficult decisions, and she would consider what they said.

That night, Rasheeda called Peyton and told her what she and Joellel had told the coach.

"Really?" a shocked Peyton replied. "Do you think coach will do it?"

"I'm not sure. She said she would think about it," Rasheeda answered.

The two girls talked for a while longer, discussing everything from the events that took place at practice that day to how they thought Addison would take the news.

Peyton entered practice the next day with trepidation. *Is coach going to replace Addison? Has Coach spoken with Addison? What's going to happen today after the way Addison left practice yesterday?* When Peyton left the locker room and headed to the practice floor, she noticed that neither Coach Anderson nor Addison were anywhere to be seen. Coach Havers was talking with players and supervising.

After a few moments, Coach Havers blew the whistle. "Okay, everyone. Let's get started with stretching and warmups."

They always started practice with stretching and warmups. The only difference was that Addison and Coach Anderson were missing. After the team had completed its customary beginning-of-practice routine, Coach Anderson walked through the gymnasium door. In unison, the girls stopped what they were doing and turned toward their coach.

"Gather around," Coach said. "As you all know, there were some issues at practice yesterday. Just now, I spoke with Addison and explained to her that she would be suspended three games for her actions and attitude towards her team and coaches. I then informed Addison that Peyton is now the starter. Addison has decided that she doesn't feel comfortable in that role and has chosen to leave the team."

The Holland girls looked at coach and then at each other in utter shock and amazement. No one could believe what had just transpired. Not only was Peyton replacing Addison, but Addison was no longer on the team. Practice continued, but it was obvious that things were different. It was clear that the girls were still recovering from the day's earlier events.

After practice, Coach Anderson asked Peyton to meet her in the coach's room to talk.

"Peyton, I am very pleased about the effort that you have given this team so far. I know you were disappointed in your role to this point in the season, but you never hung your head, you never quit, and you continued to work hard. That tells me that you have what it takes to be successful in your basketball career and in life.

"You remind me of myself as a player. You're undersized but quick, determined, and smart—not to mention that you play fearlessly and have tremendous heart. You are now the starter, and as point guard, you need to be one of the leaders on the court. You were the backup to Addison, but with her departure, you will now play the entire game because we have no one to back you up. Are you ready for this new role?"

Peyton looked her coach in the eyes and with purpose answered, "Yes, Coach, I'm ready." With that, Coach Anderson smiled and told Peyton to head home.

When Peyton entered her father's car, she couldn't contain her excitement. "Dad, you'll never guess what happened today!"

For the remainder of the car ride home, Peyton told her father about Addison quitting, Coach telling her that she's now the starter, and about how she will play the entire game now because there is no backup.

After listening quietly, Peyton's father responded, "Your mom and I have always tried to instill in you that hard work will pay off, and this is a wonderful example. No matter what happens, you just keep working hard and eventually you will have your shot. And, sweetie, you worked hard, kept your mouth shut, and now you have the opportunity to help your team win. You should be very proud of yourself."

By now they were in the driveway. Peyton gave her father a hug and ran in the house to tell her mom the good news.

CHAPTER 13

Holland Middle School's record stood at one win and two losses. With only five games remaining, there was still time to win enough games to earn a spot in the county playoffs. Holland's next opponent was Whitman Middle. Whitman's record was 2-1, with its only loss being to Brookfield.

With the Whitman game only a day away, there wasn't much practice time for Peyton and her teammates to adjust to their new circumstances. Coach Anderson wasted no time and spent the entire practice making sure Peyton knew where to position herself during all the offensive and defensive plays. After practice, Peyton felt confident and prepared for the game. She knew that the team was counting on her, and she had no intention of letting them down.

That night, Peyton was so excited that she found it hard to sleep. She lay in bed visualizing herself leading the team to victory until she finally she drifted off to sleep.

The next school day was an absolute blur to Peyton. The only thing on her mind was the game against Whitman. She even spent her lunch shooting baskets in the school gymnasium. Peyton wanted to make sure she was ready. During warmups, Peyton felt strong and confident. Her jump shot was falling through the hoop, and her legs felt loose. She couldn't wait to hear her name called during the announcement of the starting lineups. She sat on the bench with nervous anticipation waiting for her turn to run out to half court to meet her other starting teammates.

The first player announced was Rasheeda, then Joellel, then Sasha, and then the announcer bellowed, "At point guard, Peyton Washburn!" Peyton stood, legs slightly wobbling, and ran out towards center court with a look of determination.

After a brief team meeting at half court, the players took their positions around the center court circle, and the referee threw the ball in the air at center court, signaling the start of the game. From the opening tip, nothing went well for Peyton and the team. The first time down court, Peyton attempted to penetrate into the lane and then pass out to Rasheeda. The problem was that Rasheeda wasn't where Peyton passed the ball. Turnover.

The next time down court, Peyton signaled flex but dribbled to the wrong side of the court. The play immediately fell apart. The confusion and inconsistent play between Peyton and her teammates continued throughout the first half, and the score at half was Whitman 25, Holland 11.

At halftime, Coach Anderson attempted a few minor adjustments, primarily on defense, but the second half wasn't much better than the first. Players were missing easy shots, there was little communication on offense and defense, and Peyton continued making poor decisions and turning the ball over to Whitman. The final score was Whitman Middle 44, Holland 29.

Later that evening, Peyton sat in her bedroom staring at her wall. *What happened today?* she wondered. *It all went so bad.* Just then she heard a knock on her bedroom door.

"Come in."

"Peyton," her father said in a quiet but loving voice, "you ok, sweetie?"

"Yeah, I'm alright, Dad. What happened out there? I was terrible. We, as a team, were terrible."

Her father sat on the bed and put his hand on his daughter's leg. "Sometimes things just don't go the way you plan. I know you wanted to play a perfect game and show everyone that you belong as a starter. You make one mistake, then another, then another. Before you know it, things get out of control. It happens to everyone. You can't dwell on what went wrong. Just put this game behind you and move on. The team needs you, and there are still four games left in the season." Peyton nodded her head. "Come on, sweetie, you need to get some food in your system."

Peyton closed her bedroom door and followed her father downstairs.

The next day at practice, Coach reiterated what Peyton's father had told her the night before. She told the team to forget about last night's game and focus on Sherryville, Holland's next opponent. With four days until they had to face Sherryville, Peyton and the team had plenty of time to fix the mistakes they made against Whitman and work out any confusion about plays and proper player positioning. The practices were intense but productive. Every day Peyton felt more and more confident with the plays and her teammates. Unlike the previous game, Peyton felt much more comfortable heading into this game.

Sherryville was a tall team, and Coach instructed Peyton to push the ball down court every chance she got. When addressing the team prior to the game, Coach reminded the team of their game plan.

"We can't compete with their size, but they can't stay with us in the open floor. Peyton will be looking to get the ball down court in a hurry, so everyone make sure you fill your lanes and communicate. Let's run them out of the gym!"

Coach's game plan was perfect. Sherryville's starting center and power forward stood six feet three and six feet four, but they were slow. Joellel and Emily did a magnificent job of positioning themselves to grab rebounds and outletting the ball to Peyton. Rasheeda and Sasha sprinted down court, and Peyton made nearly flawless passes for easy layups and short jump shots. By the time the game was over, the center and power forward on Sherryville were bent over in exhaustion, and the final score was Holland 55, Sherryville 32.

Peyton scored twelve points, but more importantly dished out ten assists and had only one turnover. Unlike the last game, the atmosphere in the locker room after the Sherryville win was a joyful place. The girls were slapping high fives, laughing and reminiscing about shots and scores from the game. Peyton knew she played well and felt as if a weight was lifted off her shoulders.

"Gather round, girls," Coach Anderson announced. "Now that's the way we play Holland basketball! Every single one of you executed the game plan flawlessly. We have improved our record to two and three, and with three games left, we still have an opportunity to get some more wins and make the playoffs. Great job out there. Get showered and dressed, and I'll see you Monday for practice."

Peyton sat on the bench in the locker room next to Rasheeda. "Hey, Sheed, let's win the next three and get into playoffs."

Rasheeda looked back at Peyton and said, "I'm with ya. Meet me back at my house Sunday afternoon. We'll practice shooting and running the plays."

The following Monday, practice took on a whole new purpose. The Holland team knew they needed to continue winning, but the girls also seemed to be enjoying each other more, and their comfortableness was evident on the court as well. Plays were being run with no mistakes, and there was communication and support from all thirteen girls. Coach rarely had to stop practice and correct mistakes. It was as if the win versus Sherryville created an entirely new team. Peyton felt more and more comfortable as well and began executing the plays perfectly time and time again. With Peyton Washburn now running the point guard position, the Holland Middle School girls' basketball team had been transformed.

CHAPTER 14

Their next opponent was Round Rock Middle School. Round Rock was undefeated to this point in the season. It had lost to Brookfield in last year's championship game and returned all the starters from a year ago. They were big, strong, fast, and aggressive. Coach Anderson and Coach Havers had stressed all week long that, in order to win the game, Holland was going to have to be tougher than Brookfield.

As Peyton walked onto the court awaiting the jump ball, she couldn't help but notice how imposing the Round Rock girls were. *I'm just gonna have to be tougher than them,* she told herself. Any doubt of whether or not Peyton and the Holland team could play with Round Rock was settled in the first quarter. The Holland girls lead 15-14 at the quarter break, and they had yet to play their best basketball.

"Keep moving the ball on offense. We're doing a great job on that side of the ball, but, ladies, we need to be more aggressive on the defensive end," Coach pleaded. "I want to set up a full court press to begin the second quarter. Joellel is going to be the trap man, and, Peyton, I want you to set up behind the three-quarter court line and release when you see the ball getting ready to be reversed."

Holland did exactly what coach wanted, and Peyton stole four consecutive passes, which lead to eight straight Holland points. Round Rock immediately called a time out with the score 23-14. For the remainder of the half, Coach Anderson had the girls press after made baskets and drop back into a zone after missed baskets. Round Rock struggled to find a rhythm, and the score at halftime was Holland 34, Round Rock 21.

Although Holland enjoyed a comfortable lead at half, Round Rock started the second half on an 8-0 run, due in large part to their overall size advantage. They grabbed offensive rebounds and outmuscled Holland players for easy scores. It was evident that Round Rock was beginning to wear down the smaller Holland team.

"Rasheeda! I'm gonna isolate you on the wing. I'll fake a pass, and you go backdoor. We've got to stop this run!" Peyton hollered after a dead ball out of bounds.

Peyton dribbled to the left side of the court and yelled out, "One up, one up," the play for an isolation. Rasheeda darted out to the wing, with the defender close behind, and with a quick stop, Rasheeda pivoted and sprinted toward the basket, where she found a perfectly placed bounce pass from Peyton. Rasheeda stretched out her hand and laid the ball up toward the rim. As the ball left her outstretched hand, the center for Round Rock, who had rotated over to help her beaten teammate, slammed her body into Rasheeda's side just as the ball bounced off the backboard and fell through the net. The Holland bench erupted in excitement, but the excitement soon faded as they saw Rasheeda lying on the ground clutching her ankle.

"Sheed, Sheed! You alright?" Peyton yelled with obvious concern.

"I don't know. My ankle is killing me," Rasheeda muttered back, eyes closed in obvious pain.

After a few minutes of uncertainty, Coach Anderson and Coach Havers escorted Rasheeda off the basketball court and onto the bench, where she continued to writhe in pain. Coach

Havers immediately untied Rasheeda's sneaker and placed a bag of ice around her already swollen ankle. In the meantime, Coach Anderson was busy trying to adjust the game plan without her best player.

"Rasheeda is done for the game, so we have to step it up as a whole and get this win," Coach Anderson pleaded, staring at each member of her team. "Cassandra will fill in for Rasheeda."

Cassandra was a seldom-used player, primarily because she played Rasheeda's position and Rasheeda rarely left the game. Cassandra was quick and a decent shooter.

As the Holland team left the huddle, Coach Anderson grabbed Peyton by the arm. "I know you have been deferring to the others and getting them shots, and that's what a good point guard is supposed to do, but with Rasheeda down, you need to score. Do you understand me?"

Peyton looked at her coach and nodded.

With the score 36-29, Cassandra stepped to the free throw line to take Rasheeda's additional foul shot. After making the shot, the Holland lead was extended to 37-29 with four minutes remaining in the third quarter. As the period progressed, Holland struggled scoring without Rasheeda on the floor, and by the end of the third, the score was tied at 37-37.

Peyton knew that Holland needed to win this game if there was any chance at playoffs and decided that she was going to have to become more offensive minded. As soon as she touched the ball in the fourth quarter, she dribbled to the top of the three-point line, faked as if she was going one way, and quickly spun 180 degrees around the opposite direction, losing her defender. With her defender on her hip, Peyton dribbled to the foul line, where she set her feet, squared her shoulders, and let go a high-arching shot over the nearest defender. *Swish.* Holland regained the lead.

After Holland stopped Round Rock on defense, Peyton retrieved the ball from Joellel and dribbled up court. This time Peyton dribbled to the left side, then bounced the ball between her legs and changed direction in a split second, catching her defender off balance. Peyton penetrated towards the basket and shot the ball. The ball floated, bounced off the front rim, back rim, and gently fell through the hoop. Round Rock immediately called timeout, and as the Holland team jogged toward their bench, they could hear the Round Rock coach screaming at her team to stop the fourth grader. Peyton couldn't help but smile. *Fourth grader. They haven't seen anything yet.*

As the fourth quarter progressed, Round Rock began using two defenders to attempt to stop Peyton's penetration, but every time she saw two defenders approach her, she easily passed the ball to an array of open teammates, and the Holland team slowly began extending its lead. By the end of the game, the final score was Holland 56, Round Rock 43. Although the girls were ecstatic, the celebration was short-lived once the news about Rasheeda was known. Severely sprained ankle. Out indefinitely!

"Dad, what does it mean? Indefinitely?" Peyton inquired the moment she got home.

"It means that she's out for as long as it takes to get healthy," her dad responded. "Is that what Coach said about Rasheeda?"

"Yeah. We have only two games left, and we probably need to win them both to make playoffs. I don't think she is going to be able to play. Her ankle was huge and black and blue," Peyton said with obvious concern in her voice.

"Sometimes severely sprained ankles are worse than breaks, so it sounds like you're right. Rasheeda probably won't be back, but you never know," Dad replied with forced optimism.

"With Rasheeda out, I'm going to have to score more. Coach wants me to. She told me that during the game."

"If Coach wants you to score more, than score more, sweetie. Your mom and I are so impressed with how you have handled yourself throughout this entire basketball ordeal. You've amazed us time and time again by your play on the court and your attitude off the court."

Peyton hugged her father and ventured into the living room to watch TV.

CHAPTER 15

The following Monday while the team was getting warmed up for the day's practice, Rasheeda limped onto the practice floor, crutches under each arm and an air cast wrapped around her ankle. Before Peyton even had the opportunity to ask her how bad it was, Rasheeda, already knowing what Peyton and the rest of her teammates were curious about, blurted out, "I'm done! The doctor says I can't play anymore this season." Rasheeda stared at her teammates as they watched her stand there supported by her only good leg.

Peyton walked over and embraced Rasheeda with a giant hug. "I'm sorry" was all she could whisper at that moment.

The rest of the team followed Peyton's lead, and before she knew it, there was a giant huddle around Rasheeda. Coach finally blew her whistle and the team returned their focus back to practice. Rasheeda stayed the entire practice, sitting on the bleachers watching and yelling words of encouragement.

After practice, Peyton wandered over and sat next to Rasheeda. "So. How frustrated are you?"

"Unbelievably," Rasheeda answered. "We only have two games left that we need to win, and I can't even help. Couldn't have happened at a worse time.

"I know," said Peyton.

"Hey, Peyton. You realize that you have to start scoring more now. The team can't win unless you shoot more."

"Yeah, Coach said the same thing to me the other day when you went down."

"Did coach give you any specifics on how she wanted you to score more? You know, jump shots or penetration?" Rasheeda inquired.

"No, she just said score more. I guess I'll have to feel out the game and see what the other team is giving me."

"Well, all I know is that I still want to make playoffs, whether I can play or not, so promise me you'll win these next two games!" pleaded Rasheeda.

"I promise."

With that, Peyton helped Rasheeda up and onto her crutches, and they both headed for the locker room door.

Holland's next opponent was Sandy Pond Middle School. Sandy Pond didn't have a very good record, but this was Holland's first game without Rasheeda, and there was no telling how the team would perform. Sandy Pond's best player was their center. Her name was Carrie, and she was the biggest player in the league, standing six feet five inches tall and weighing two hundred pounds. She also had the reputation of being a bully. If Holland was to win the game, not only did Peyton have to score, but Joellel was also going to have to stop Carrie.

Cassandra was starting in place of Rasheeda, along with Peyton, Joellel, Emily, and Sasha. Peyton knew from the opening tip that she was going to have to score. She had to change her mindset from passer first to scorer first. Standing at center court awaiting the jump ball signifying the start of the game, Peyton felt different. The normal butterflies in her stomach weren't there. She felt calm, relaxed, and focused.

Bleep! The whistle from the referee blew and the ball was thrown in the air. Joellel leaped and reached the ball at its highest point and tipped it to Cassandra. Peyton, seeing the play develop immediately, sprinted toward the basket, and Cassandra fired a chest pass to Peyton in perfect rhythm. Peyton snatched the ball, took three dribbles, and outstretched her hand toward the rim. As she released the ball from her hand, she felt a slap to the side of her head. The last thing Peyton saw before falling to the ground was the ball sailing in the air. As Peyton lay on the ground dazed and confused, she heard cheering and clapping. She turned to see Rasheeda, Coach Anderson, and Coach Havers standing and clapping from the bench. The ball had gone through the basket and Peyton was headed to the foul line for a possible three-point play.

As Emily helped Peyton off the floor, Carrie, the center for Sandy Pond, strolled over, and as she passed Peyton and Emily whispered, "Every time you come into the lane, I'm gonna hit you harder and harder."

Peyton and Emily looked at each other with bewilderment and then at the opposing center who had a grin on her face. Peyton calmly walked toward the free throw line, gathered herself, and made the free throw. Peyton and the Holland basketball team, leading 3-0, ran back down court and set up their defense.

The first time Sandy Pond was on offense, they passed the ball to Carrie, who had pushed Joellel all the way under the basket. Carrie received a lob pass from her point guard, turned, and laid the ball in the basket with little resistance from an outsized Joellel. Holland 3, Sandy Pond 2.

Peyton received the inbound pass and headed back down court for Holland's second opportunity on offense. From the moment Peyton received the ball, she had no intention of passing it. There was no way Carrie, or anyone else for that matter, was going to intimidate her. Upon crossing mid court, Peyton yelled, "Iso one, Iso one," which was the play call for an isolation for the point guard.

Peyton teammates spread to the far sides of the court, and Peyton dribbled the ball from her right hand to her left hand, back and forth toward her defender in a sort of rhythmic manner. Peyton stared at her defender, waiting for the opportunity to rush past. Then, when she saw her defender attempt to adjust her body for a better defensive position, she bolted past her and towards the hoop. Just as Peyton expected, Carrie had rotated over for defensive help, and Peyton threw her body into Carrie's and slammed to the floor for the second time in as many trips down court.

As Peyton began to rise from the court, Carrie stood over her and reiterated what she had said the last time Peyton had gone into the lane. "I told you I was going to hit you harder and harder!"

Peyton looking at Carrie, just smiled and walked back to the free throw line for two more free throw attempts. After sinking both free throws, the score was now 5-2, and Sandy Pond was back in control of the ball.

Sandy Pond again set a play and passed the ball to Carrie in the post. Carrie turned and threw a jump hook over the outstretched hand of Joellel. Two points. Holland 5, Sandy Pond 4.

Peyton once again took the inbounds pass and headed down court. Once again as she crossed mid court she yelled, "Iso one, Iso one!"

Again, Peyton's teammates spread the floor, and Peyton again set up her defender and waited for the opportunity to beat her to the rim. This time Peyton used the inside-out move. This was a move her father had taught her in her driveway. She dribbled the ball with her right hand and made a movement as if she was going to cross the ball back to her left hand, but instead she kept the ball in her right hand and jetted past her defender, who was helplessly off balance. As Peyton entered the foul lane, there once again was Carrie, grin and all. Peyton leaped in the air and lofted the ball towards the rim, just as Carrie's forearm came slamming down on Peyton's shoulder. The ball rolled around the rim and fell out.

Peyton rose from the floor, and as she headed back to the free throw line, Carrie approached her and issued her third consecutive threat. "Hey, you don't get it, shorty. I told you I'm gonna keep on hitting you, so stay out of my lane!"

This time as Peyton looked at Carrie, she couldn't help but respond, "Hey, Carrie, you see that teammate of yours at the scorer's table? She's there because you have three fouls in the first three minutes of the game and your coach is replacing you. Now, go have a seat and watch me continue to get into *your* lane!"

As Peyton walked toward the free throw line, she overheard the Sandy Pond coach arguing with Carrie. Peyton couldn't hear exactly what was being said, but she knew the coach was frustrated with his player.

Shortly after Carrie exited the game, Holland scored twelve consecutive points, opening up a 17-4 lead by the end of the first quarter, with Peyton having scored ten of those points.

At the quarter break, Peyton couldn't help but notice the gigantic grin on Rasheeda's face. After Coach Anderson finished her strategy talk and game plan for the remainder of the game, Peyton and her teammates stood and prepared to reenter the game for the second quarter. Peyton once again looked at Rasheeda, who still possessed the grin she had displayed earlier.

"You're something else, you know that, Peyton?" said an amused Rasheeda.

"Hey, we need to win these last two games to make the playoffs. Getting into someone's head is part of the game."

Peyton, feeling good about her response, winked at Rasheeda and turned toward the court. The Sandy Pond coach had no choice but to have Carrie reenter the game in the second quarter. The game was already getting out of reach, and Carrie was the only player on Sandy Pond who stood a chance of changing the momentum Holland currently enjoyed.

During the quarter intermission, Coach Anderson had instructed her team that in the case of Carrie's return to the game, Emily would be helping Joellel double-team Carrie. This strategy proved to be effective. The first time Sandy Pond received the ball in the second quarter, Joellel stood behind Carrie while Emily stood in front. Although Carrie was defended extremely well, the Sandy Pond players still attempted to try and get Carrie the ball. This proved beneficial for Holland. Three consecutive times down court, Holland stole the ball on an attempted pass to Carrie and scored on the opposite end of the court.

Holland continued to double-team Carrie the remainder of the game, and Peyton continued to be aggressive on offense. When the final buzzer indicated the end of the game, the scoreboard read Holland 58, Sandy Pond 30. Peyton's stat sheet read 28 points, 8 assists, 4 steals, and only 3 turnovers.

As Peyton walked toward the locker room, Coach Anderson walked along her side. "You did exactly what we needed you to do. You were aggressive, and not only did that get us the points we needed, but it also got Carrie in foul trouble. We need you to be that aggressive one more game."

Peyton looked at her coach and smiled. She knew she was going to have to be just as productive, if not more, in the next game if there was any chance to make the playoffs.

CHAPTER 16

The final game of the regular season was in three days, and the Holland girls knew that it was going to be their most difficult. They were scheduled to play Perryville Middle School. Perryville was currently in second place with a 6-1 record, its only loss coming to Brookfield Middle School on a last second shot. Holland had played Brookfield the first game of the season with a healthy Rasheeda and lost by eighteen points, so beating Perryville without Rasheeda was going to be very challenging.

Peyton was feeling extremely anxious leading up to the game. She knew that she was going to have to play one of her best games in order for her team to win and make the playoffs. To calm her nerves, Peyton knew she was going to have to talk with her father. He always seemed to know exactly the right thing to say, and that comforted Peyton.

The night before the game, Peyton asked her father to come to her room so they could talk.

"Dad, do you have any advice for me for tomorrow's game? I mean, I know I have to score and help others score, but is there anything else you think I can do to help the team win?"

"Well, honey, just remember that no matter what happens tomorrow, don't allow your teammates to get down on themselves. I know you never thought you were going to have to be one of the leaders on this team, but the fact of the matter is that you *are* one of the leaders. The girls listen to you, and they're going to need you to be strong tomorrow. If you drop your head, then they will drop their heads. Lead by example."

Peyton smiled at her father, gave him a hug, and settled in for some quiet time.

The game against Perryville couldn't have begun any worse. Perryville scored on its first five possessions, while Holland struggled to score. Perryville played a suffocating defense, double-teaming Peyton every time she crossed half court with the basketball. Not only was it a struggle to get a good shot, even when there was the opportunity to score, the ball seemed to find a way to roll around the rim and fall out. Joellel, who had a size difference on her opponent, missed three easy shots, and Sasha and Emily each missed uncontested layups. After the end of a brutal first quarter of play, Holland trailed 16-6.

"We need to focus!" pleaded Coach Anderson.

"They are doubling Peyton every time she has the ball in her hands. Their game plan is to have someone else on the team beat them. Well, if that's what they want, then that's what they're going to get. If your defender leaves you to go and double-team Peyton, flash to an open area and Peyton will give you the ball. Let's settle down. The shots will fall! Let's start the second quarter with a full court press."

As the Holland team was getting ready to head back on the floor, Peyton, thinking about her talk with her father from the night before, reiterated Coach's feelings. "Come on, ladies. We haven't come this far this year to fall apart now. Let's keep on battling. We'll get back in this game!"

The press did not have the effect that Coach was hoping for. Perryville easily broke it three consecutive times and scored six quick points to take a 22-6 lead early in the second quarter. Holland continued to battle, using Joellel as their primary weapon. Joellel's size differential was key in keeping Holland in the game, but when the halftime buzzer sounded, the score was Perryville 31, Holland 18.

At half, Coach Anderson continued to stress that others were going to have to get involved if there was any chance in a comeback.

"Joellel is keeping us in the game. Keep getting the ball to her, if possible, but we also need someone on the outside to knock down a shot or two. If they continue to double-team Peyton, Sasha or Cassandra will need to find open areas and make them pay. Let's keep battling!"

Walking out of the locker room for the start of the second half, Peyton quickly pulled Cassandra aside. "They are leaving you to double me. Flash to the three-point line and I will find you. Make them pay!"

Just as Coach predicted, Perryville began the second half the same way they ended the first. As soon as Peyton crossed half court with the ball, the Perryville defender who was guarding Cassandra immediately ran to double Peyton. Peyton saw Cassandra flash to the top left side of the court by the three-point line. Peyton leaped in the air and fired a bullet pass to a waiting Cassandra, who calmly caught the ball, set her feet, and fired off a three-point shot. *Swish.*

After a defensive stop by Holland, Peyton once again crossed half court to find a double-team. Cassandra again flashed to the three-point line, where she received a pass from Peyton. *Swish.*

On Perryville's next possession, their point guard dribbled into the lane, only to find a double-team from Joellel and Emily, which lead to a forced pass and a turnover. Peyton once again dribbled the ball up court toward a waiting defender. Once again, a double-team. This time Cassandra flashed to the right side of the court, where again Peyton found her wide open. Feet set, ball in the air, *swish.*

Bleep! "Time out Perryville."

The Holland players hustled to their bench with newfound excitement. After Cassandra's three consecutive three-pointers, the score was now 31-27.

"See? Were right back in it!" screamed an excited Coach Anderson. "They are probably going to pull the double-team off Peyton, which means that, Peyton, you can now attempt to beat your defender off the dribble. Also, let's keep pounding the ball down to Joelle. They have no answer for that."

With Perryville no longer double-teaming Peyton, she took immediate advantage. "Iso one, Iso one," she yelled out after crossing half court. Peyton dribbled left, crossed the ball over quickly to her right hand, and sprinted by her defender, stretching out her hands and laying the ball over the rim. Two more points!

As the game wore on, Peyton continued to beat her defender off the dribble and score, pass the ball to Joellel for an easy basket, or pass it to Holland's latest threat, Cassandra. However, as the Holland team continued to score, so did Perryville. Back and forth the two teams went, each score placing pressure on the opposing team to keep pace.

The game see-sawed back and forth the remainder of the second half. With the score tied at 50-50 with one minute remaining on the clock, the Perryville point guard slowly dribbled the ball up court. Peyton stood in defensive position, waiting for any opportunity to try and get the ball back in her team's possession. She knew that without the ball, there was no way they could win. It was obvious that Perryville was playing for the last shot, which meant that they were going to let the clock run all the way down to a few seconds before attempting a shot. That way, the worst-case scenario for Perryville was overtime.

Peyton didn't want to take the chance in overtime. She needed that ball for her team and to make the playoffs. She closely watched the Perryville point guard, looking for any sign of complacency. With eighteen seconds left on the clock, she saw her opportunity. As the Perryville coached yelled out a play to be run and the Perryville point guard turned her head to acknowledge her coach, Peyton dashed toward her and knocked the ball loose. The ball sailed down court, and both Peyton and her opponent sprinted after the ball. Peyton, using her speed, caught the ball before it sailed out of bounds and called time out. Holland had possession with fourteen seconds left in the game.

"I'm setting up an isolation for Peyton," Coach began. "Spread out and give her room. Peyton, I want you to begin your penetration with eight seconds left. Get to the basket, and if someone comes to help out, find Joellel."

Sasha inbounded the ball to Peyton, who then stood near the half-court line dribbling the ball back and forth from right hand to left hand. The seconds on the scoreboard clock ticked away.

Twelve, eleven, ten, nine . . .

Peyton glanced at the clock and then back at her defender. With eight seconds left, she began her move. She dribbled right and then, using the move her dad had taught her in their driveway, faked as if she was going to cross over to her left hand, and then went back towards the right hand, and inside-out dribble. Her defender, thinking that she was headed left, stumbled when she realized Peyton was continuing right.

Five, four . . .

Peyton took two more dribbles and stopped at the foul line.

Three, two . . .

Peyton bent her knees, jumped in the air, and with the flick of the wrist, let the ball sail toward the rim.

One . . .

The ball fell through the rim, caressing the net as time expired.

The Holland girls' basketball team ran to Peyton, jumping and screaming in the center of the court. There was commotion and noise throughout the entire gymnasium from fans and onlookers, but the loudest roar of all could be heard coming from the girls at center court.

"Playoffs! Playoffs! Playoffs!"

Review Requested:

We'd like to know if you enjoyed the book.
Please consider leaving a review on the platform from which
you purchased the book.

CPSIA information can be obtained
at www.ICGtesting.com
Printed in the USA
BVHW031414210920
589269BV00001B/65